Melodie
the Music
Fairy

For Alice and Lara Clerc, with the
hope that they will seek out and
find lovely fairies in France.

Special thanks to
Marilyn Kaye

No part of this work may be reproduced, stored in a retrieval
system, or transmitted in any form or by any means, electronic,
mechanical, photocopying, recording, or otherwise, without written
permission of the publisher. For information regarding permission,
write to Rainbow Magic Limited c/o HIT Entertainment,
830 South Greenville Avenue, Allen, TX 75002-3320.

ISBN 978-0-545-22169-6

12 11 10 9 8 7 6 5 4   12 13 14 15/0

Printed in the U.S.A.   40

First Scholastic Printing, July 2010

Melodie
the Music
Fairy

by Daisy Meadows

J
FIC
Meadows
2010
VOL 2

SCHOLASTIC INC.

New York   Toronto   London   Auckland
Sydney   Mexico City   New Delhi   Hong Kong

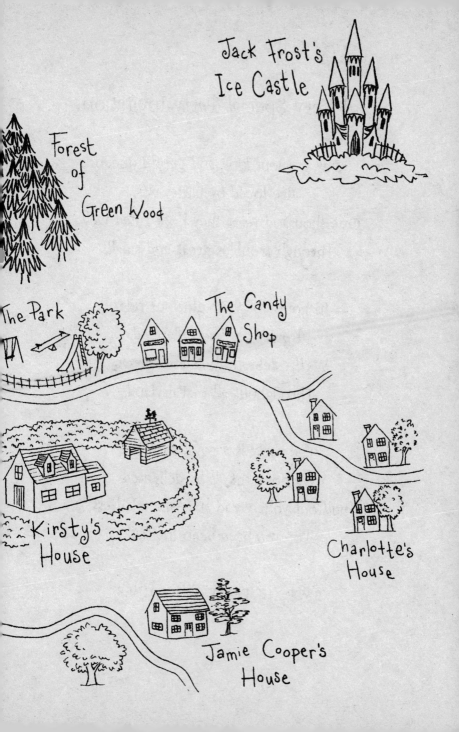

A Very Special Party Invitation

Our gracious king and gentle queen
Are loved by fairies all.
One thousand years they have ruled well,
Through troubles great and small.

In honor of their glorious reign
A party has been planned.
We'll celebrate their anniversary
Throughout all of Fairyland.

The party is a royal surprise,
We hope they'll be delighted.
So pull out your wand and fanciest dress . . .
For *you* have been invited!

RSVP: THE FAIRY GODMOTHER

Contents

Musical Mayhem

"Kirsty, you're an amazing dancer!"
Rachel Walker smiled, clapping her hands
as her friend took a bow. Kirsty had
just finished practicing the ballet steps
she would be performing later that
evening.

"It will look even better tonight, when
I'm with the other dancers and everyone
is in costume," Kirsty replied with a grin.

"And wait until you hear the beautiful music."

Rachel was staying with her best friend, Kirsty Tate, for the week. That evening, the girls were going to the village hall for a very special occasion—the first anniversary of Kirsty's ballet school.

"It's going to be a great party," Kirsty went on. "My ballet teacher decorated the hall and is organizing some games,

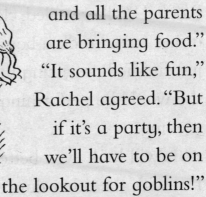

and all the parents are bringing food."

"It sounds like fun," Rachel agreed. "But if it's a party, then we'll have to be on the lookout for goblins!"

Kirsty nodded. She and Rachel shared a

magical secret: They were friends with the fairies! But right now, there were problems in Fairyland, and Kirsty and Rachel had promised to help.

The fairies were planning a surprise celebration for the 1000th anniversary of the fairy king and queen's rule. It would be taking place in five days, and the Party Fairies were in charge of making it as special as possible using their party bags of magic fairy dust.

But nasty Jack Frost had other plans. Banished to his ice castle by the fairy king and queen, he had decided to throw a party of his own on the very same day! Jack Frost knew that whenever a party in the human world went wrong, the Party Fairies would fly to the rescue. So he had sent his goblins to ruin as many human parties as possible. Then, they would grab the fairies' party bags when the fairies flew in to set things straight. Jack Frost wanted the fairy magic to make his party spectacular. Without magic, the anniversary celebration would be ruined!

Suddenly, the girls heard Mrs. Tate's voice. "Time to go, girls!" she called.

Kirsty and Rachel hurried downstairs to join Kirsty's mom and dad.

Mr. Tate held up a cake tin. "I made

cupcakes for
the party,"
he explained,
lifting the lid.
"Cupcakes,
my favorite!"
Rachel said
with delight.

"You couldn't have made anything
better."

"Thanks, Dad," Kirsty grinned,
carefully taking the tin.

Mr. Tate drove them all to the village
hall. When they arrived, it was already full
of friends and families who had come to
join the celebration.

"The hall looks so different!" Kirsty
gasped. Rows of chairs had been set
up to face the stage, just like in a real

theater. Shiny silver streamers hung from the ceiling, twinkling Christmas lights bordered the stage, and bunches of silver and white balloons floated above each table of food.

While Mr. and Mrs. Tate chatted with

other parents, Rachel and Kirsty arranged the cupcakes on a plate. They weren't the only things that looked delicious.

"Yum, chocolate éclairs!" Kirsty pointed out. Then she frowned. "They look almost too good to be true."

"Maybe we should test some of these—just to make sure the food hasn't been spoiled by a goblin!" Rachel suggested.

Kirsty nodded. She took an éclair, and Rachel ate one of Mr. Tate's cupcakes. Then the girls smiled at each other—the treats were delicious. No goblins had been anywhere near this party food!

Just then, the ballet teacher, Miss Kelly, joined them. "Kirsty, it's time for you to go and get ready now," she said. "And you must be Rachel," she added with a smile. "Kirsty said you would be coming."

"Can I help Kirsty and the other girls get ready?" Rachel asked eagerly.

Miss Kelly nodded. "Thank you, Rachel. I could certainly use another pair of hands."

Kirsty led the way to the dressing room, which was behind the stage. While the dancers slipped into their tights and tutus, Rachel helped Miss Kelly apply rosy powder to the girls' cheeks and a dab of pink gloss to their lips. Finally, the dancers put on their ballet shoes. They tied the pink satin ribbons firmly around their ankles.

There was a feeling of excitement
in the air as the audience took their
seats. Watching from backstage, Rachel
breathed a sigh of relief. The decorations,
food, and costumes were all perfect. It
looked like Jack Frost's goblins hadn't
heard about the ballet-school party,
after all!

Miss Kelly walked onto the stage. "Ladies
and gentlemen, I am pleased to present
our very first class of ballerinas. They will
perform for you tonight in honor of our

school's anniversary," she announced.

The audience clapped as Miss Kelly hurried into the wings. Then the curtain rose, and the music began.

With their arms held gracefully over their heads, the dancers ran daintily onto the stage. She'd seen Kirsty practice, so Rachel knew what was coming next. But she hadn't seen the dance with the costumes and music. The girls all looked as beautiful as fairies in their pretty tulle tutus!

But suddenly, the music changed. It seemed to speed up, and the dancers started to have trouble staying in time. Although they kept dancing, Rachel could see from Kirsty's face that something was wrong.

She watched in dismay as one or two of the girls stumbled. They stubbed their toes on the stage as they tried to spin and leap more quickly.

The music was still getting faster and 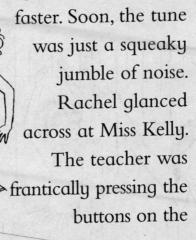 faster. Soon, the tune was just a squeaky jumble of noise. Rachel glanced across at Miss Kelly. The teacher was frantically pressing the buttons on the

CD player, but it wasn't
making any difference. The
dancers whirled and spun
more and more quickly,
but it was impossible
for them to keep up
with the music. Two
dancers bumped into each
other, and another tripped over her own
feet.

"I can't stop the CD player!" Miss Kelly
gasped. "I don't know what's wrong."

But Rachel knew. She was sure that this
was the work of one of Jack Frost's sneaky
goblins!

The Trembling Tambourine

The girls stopped dancing and rushed offstage. A couple of the parents came, too, to help Miss Kelly with the music. But nobody seemed to know what was wrong with the CD player.

"This is definitely the work of goblins!" Rachel said under her breath. She looked for Kirsty, but couldn't see her

in the crowd of people backstage. "Well,
I'm going to find him and stop his
tricks!"

Rachel glanced around the village
hall, and her heart sank. She could see
lots of places where a goblin might hide.
Backstage, there were trunks and racks
of costumes, plus the big cardboard
set from the last performance—not to
mention two dressing rooms, a music
room, and a tiny office.

But then, just as Rachel was
wondering where to start looking,
she saw a pile of
musical instruments
stacked in the
wings on the
other side
of the stage.
One of the
instruments, a
tambourine,
was shaking—all
on its own!

Rachel gulped. She could see that
there was no one on that side of the
stage, and none of the other instruments
were moving. She knew the tambourine
was too small to hide a goblin, but what
would make it shake like that? *Could a*

goblin have brushed past it? she wondered.
And could the goblin still be over there?

Quietly, Rachel slipped across the stage
to the other side. She tiptoed toward the
stack of instruments, looking around in
case the goblin was hiding nearby. She
wanted to spot him
before he spotted her!
But she couldn't see
anything suspicious.
With her heart
pounding, she knelt
down beside the
tambourine. Very carefully,
Rachel lifted it with one finger.
As she did, a golden light glowed from
under the rim.

Rachel grinned and eagerly lifted the

tambourine all the way. She had already
guessed what she would find. Sure
enough, a tiny, shimmering fairy was
sitting there, with her face buried in her
hands.

"You're a
Party Fairy!"
Rachel exclaimed
with delight.

The fairy
raised her head.
She was sobbing so
hard that she had
been making the
tambourine bells
jingle. Her tears shimmered in the light
like tiny diamonds as they rolled down
her cheeks. "That's right, I'm Melodie

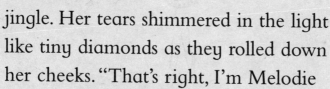

the Music Fairy." She sniffed as she adjusted her pink headband. "And you must be Rachel."

Melodie stood on tiptoe. She was wearing a beautiful pink dress, with black music notes around the hem. Her golden hair was in braids that swung as she turned her head.

"Where's Kirsty?" Melodie asked.

"She's not far away," Rachel told her. "But why are you crying?"

Melodie wiped away a last sparkling tear. "I came to fix the music," she explained. "If I had known one of those nasty goblins was to blame, I would have been more careful."

Rachel frowned. "Was a goblin waiting for you?"

"Yes," Melodie wailed. "He grabbed my party bag and ran off with it. Now I can't fix the music for the ballet. And if I don't get my party bag back, there won't be any music for the king and queen's anniversary party, either!"

Melodie's Mission

Rachel felt very sorry for Melodie. "Don't worry," she said. "Kirsty and I will help you get your party bag back."

Melodie brightened immediately. "Oh, do you mean it?" she cried.

Rachel smiled. "Of course I do," she replied. "Now let's go and find Kirsty."

Quickly, Melodie picked up her

glittering wand and fluttered into the pocket of Rachel's skirt. Then Rachel made her way back toward the people gathered around the CD player.

Kirsty spotted her friend coming across the stage, and hurried to meet her. "Rachel, I think I know what happened to the music," Kirsty whispered in her ear. "It's goblin trouble!"

Rachel nodded. "Look!" she said, and
held her skirt pocket open so Kirsty
could peek inside.

Melodie waved at
her. "Hello, Kirsty.
I'm Melodie the
Music Fairy,"
she called in her
soft voice.

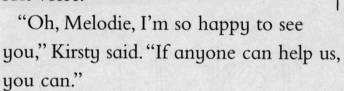

"Oh, Melodie, I'm so happy to see
you," Kirsty said. "If anyone can help us,
you can."

"She came here to fix the music,"
Rachel explained. "But a goblin stole
her party bag."

Kirsty's face fell. "Oh, no!" She groaned.
"We have to get it back before the
goblin escapes and takes it to Jack
Frost!"

Melodie nodded eagerly. "But where should we start looking?" she asked.

Rachel thought for a moment. "There are so many people in the main hall, I don't think he would risk hanging around there," she said. "Let's check the other rooms backstage."

With all the noise and confusion, the

girls were able to slip away without being noticed. They hurried along the backstage hallway, and ran into the ladies' dressing room. Rachel looked in the lockers where the dancers had left their clothes, while Kirsty checked the closets and searched through the costumes. There was no sign of a goblin.

♪ ♫ ♪ ♪ ♫ ♪ ♪ ♫ ♪

Next, they tried the office. Melodie
flew out of Rachel's pocket to check
under the desk, Rachel looked out
the window, and Kirsty opened all the
drawers in the filing cabinet. There were
papers and folders everywhere, but no
goblin.

The three friends returned to the hallway feeling a little glum.

"Do you think he's already gone?" Rachel asked.

Melodie shook her head. "He wouldn't have gotten out with so many people around," she replied. "He must be hiding somewhere until the coast is clear."

Suddenly, Kirsty frowned. "I can hear something!" she exclaimed, listening closely. "Someone's playing the piano."

Now Rachel could hear it, too, very faintly. "Maybe someone is practicing in the music room," she suggested.

"But who would practice the piano

while a party's going on?" asked Kirsty.

Rachel listened again. "Well, whoever it is, they certainly need the practice," she said, making a face. "It sounds terrible!"

Melodie's eyes lit up. "Only a goblin could play that badly!" she cried. Immediately, she zoomed off toward the sound. The girls ran after her. As they got closer to the music room, the jangling sound of the piano grew louder.

They found the door cracked open, and peeked cautiously into the room. They could hear the terrible music clearly now, and they could even see the piano standing in the middle of the floor. But to their surprise, there was nobody playing it!

Goblin Discovered

The girls stared at the piano in amazement. Even Melodie looked confused. But then Kirsty had an idea. "Maybe the goblin's hiding *inside* the piano!" she said. "He could be playing it from there."

"Let's all go and look," Rachel suggested.

"No, let me go," Kirsty replied. "Ballet shoes are soft. If the goblin is in there, he won't hear me coming."

"Good idea," Rachel agreed. If the goblin was hiding in the piano, they didn't want to give him any warning.

Kirsty slipped through the open door and tiptoed over to the piano. Holding her breath, she carefully lifted the lid and peeked inside.

And there he was—a tiny, nasty-looking goblin, laughing gleefully and

running up and down the piano
strings, with Melodie's party
bag swinging from
one hand.
As he ran, he sang
to himself in a
croaky voice:
"I've got the
fairy's bag, I'm
such a smarty.
I'll take it to
Jack Frost, and
he'll throw a
party!"
Very gently, Kirsty lowered
the piano lid. Then she turned to the
door and nodded at her friends.
"What do we do now?" Rachel
whispered to Melodie. "How are we

going to get your party bag back?"

Melodie frowned thoughtfully, as
Rachel looked around the room. There
was a set of drums not far from the
piano, and on one of the drums lay a
pair of cymbals. They gave Rachel an
idea! "See those cymbals?" she said,
pointing them out to Melodie. "Do you
think you could lift one?"

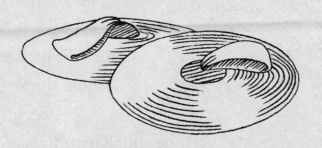

"I think so," Melodie replied, looking
at Rachel curiously.

"Great! I'll take the other one," Rachel
said.

"But how will you get over there to pick it up?" Melodie asked. "If you walk across the room, the goblin might hear you coming."

"Not if I'm a fairy . . ." Rachel smiled. Melodie nodded and waved her wand. A cloud of glittering fairy dust showered down on Rachel, and she felt herself shrinking.

By the time the dust had settled, Rachel was as tiny as Melodie. She fluttered her wings happily and flew around in a little circle. Then she flitted across the music room, with Melodie close behind.

The cymbals were heavy! Melodie and
Rachel both had to struggle
to lift them, but at last
they managed it.

They flew over to
Kirsty, who had
been watching them in
confusion. Rachel whispered
in Kirsty's ear so the goblin wouldn't
hear.

"When I wink, open the lid of the piano," she said.

Kirsty nodded, wondering what Rachel was planning.

Rachel and Melodie held up the cymbals and hovered in the air, face to face. Then Rachel winked at Kirsty, who immediately lifted the piano lid. At the same moment, Rachel and Melodie rushed toward each other. With a crash that shook the room, the cymbals clashed together—right above the goblin's head!

A New Problem

The goblin let out a loud scream, clapped his hands over his ears, and dropped Melodie's party bag. "What a horrible noise!" he shrieked in surprise. "My head aches!" He jumped out of the piano and ran out of the room at top speed.

Rachel smiled. She agreed that the cymbals had made a deafening noise, but at least she and Melodie had been ready for it. She heard a smaller crash. When she looked around, she saw that Melodie had dropped her cymbal and swooped into the piano to grab her party bag.

"Ooh, that was fun!" Melodie exclaimed. "The goblin escaped, but I have my party bag back, and that's all that matters." She opened the bag and peeked inside. As she did, some golden, glittering music notes drifted out. "And it's still full of magic fairy dust," she declared happily.

At that moment, Kirsty heard footsteps in the hallway outside. "Someone's coming," she whispered. "Quick, you two, hide in the piano!"

Rachel dropped her cymbal with a clatter and flew to join Melodie inside the piano. Kirsty put the lid down quickly.

She was just in time! The door to the room swung open, and Miss Kelly came in. "Hello, Kirsty, are you all right?" she asked anxiously. "What was all that noise?"

Kirsty had to think very quickly.

"Um, I thought that there, uh, might be another CD player in this room," she explained. "I was looking for it when I knocked over the cymbals."

Miss Kelly laughed. "Well, we need you on stage now. I think we'll be able to start the ballet again in a minute. Melissa's dad is an electrician, and he's fixing the CD player."

Kirsty frowned. Could a human electrician fix a machine that was broken by a goblin? She had a feeling that only fairy magic would get that CD player working again. And she knew just who could help. But Melodie was stuck inside the piano with Rachel!

"I'll come in a minute, Miss Kelly," Kirsty said, thinking fast. "Some sequins fell off my costume. I just need to find them first."

"Your costume looks fine," the ballet teacher told her briskly. "A sequin or two makes no difference. Besides, there's no time to sew them back on, and we don't want to keep our audience waiting any longer."

Kirsty had no choice. Reluctantly, she followed Miss Kelly out of the music room, leaving Rachel and Melodie trapped inside the piano.

What would they do?

The Show Must Go On!

"Oh, no!" Rachel cried after Kirsty and Miss Kelly had left. "Who knows how long we're going to be stuck in here now?"

Melodie laughed, a tinkling musical sound. "Don't worry, Rachel," she said. With a wave of her magic wand, the piano lid flew open in a burst of sparkling fairy magic!

Rachel and Melodie flew out. As soon as Rachel reached the ground, Melodie waved her wand again and turned Rachel back to her normal size. Holding her party bag tightly, Melodie hid herself in Rachel's pocket. "We can save the party now," she said happily. "Let's go!"

As Rachel hurried out of the music room, she noticed that the squeaky, super-fast music had stopped. She wondered if the spell had been broken when the goblin ran away. Or maybe Melissa's dad had fixed the CD player, after all.

When she reached the stage, she saw a big group of people still gathered around the machine. Peeking through the crowd, Rachel caught a glimpse of Melissa's dad with a screwdriver in one hand and a pair of pliers in the other. Miss Kelly and Kirsty were by his side.

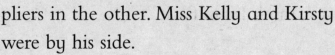

51

"What's happening?" Melodie asked from Rachel's pocket.

"I think Melissa's dad took the CD player apart," Rachel whispered. "There are bits of metal and plastic all over the floor."

"Is he going to put it back together now?" Melodie wanted to know.

"I think so," Rachel murmured. She edged a little closer to watch.

"I'm terribly sorry," the man was saying to Miss Kelly. "I've repaired CD players before, but I've never seen anything like this. I don't think I can fix it."

"Do you think *you* can fix it?" Rachel whispered to Melodie.

"Yes, I'm sure I can—with fairy magic," Melodie answered. She peeked out of Rachel's pocket and her face fell. "But not with all these people  around," she added. "Someone would see me sprinkling fairy dust over the machine."

"Maybe I can get everyone to move away," Rachel said thoughtfully. But even though she racked her brain, she

♪ ♫ ♪ ♪ ♫ ♪ ♫ ♪

couldn't think of anything that would
make the people leave the CD player.

Rachel looked around, hoping that
a brilliant thought would pop into her
head. And then she remembered the
musical instruments in the wings on the
other side of the stage, where she had
first found Melodie.

No one could see them from the CD
player. When Rachel snuck over to the
pile of instruments, she was happy to see
that there wasn't anybody else around.

Gently, she lifted the little fairy out
of her pocket. "Look," she said softly.
"I've got an idea.
Can you do anything
with these musical
instruments instead?"

Melodie smiled and
clapped her hands.

"Yes, I can!" she exclaimed.
"Is anyone looking?"

"No, we're out of sight right here,"
Rachel told her.

Quickly, Melodie fluttered over to
the instruments and perched lightly
on the violin. She took a handful of
glittering music notes from her party
bag and carefully sprinkled them over
the violin's strings.

Flitting from instrument to instrument, Melodie threw a few sparkling notes over each one. Finally, she waved her wand with an expert twirl.

At once, the bow that had been lying next to the violin floated into the air and began moving across the violin's strings.

The flute hovered as soft, sweet sounds poured from it, while it seemed like invisible fingers plucked the strings of a harp. Rachel heard the deep, low notes of a horn and watched in amazement as all the instruments began to play themselves!

From across the stage, Rachel heard Miss Kelly exclaim in surprise. "That's our ballet music!" she cried. "Where is it coming from?"

Rachel ran back to the group. "I found another CD player," she told the ballet teacher. She caught Kirsty's eye and smiled. Rachel didn't have to tell her friend that this was fairy magic at work!

"Quickly, dancers take your places," Miss Kelly called. The girls rushed onto the stage and the audience headed back to their seats.

Miss Kelly turned to Rachel. "Could you start the music from the beginning again, please?" she asked.

Rachel bit her lip. She wasn't sure that she could. What if Melodie had already gone back to Fairyland? Anxiously, she hurried back to the instruments, and then she smiled with relief. She should have known that Melodie wouldn't leave without saying

good-bye. The fairy was still there,
dancing to the music, her white dress
swirling around her.

"Can you start the music from the
beginning?" Rachel asked her.

Melodie's wand fluttered and she threw
a few more glittering music notes into
the air. The music stopped for an instant,
then began all over again.

As Kirsty and the others began to
dance, Rachel and Melodie watched

the performance
from the wings.
"Oh, it's beautiful!"
Melodie exclaimed,
copying the dancers'
graceful arm
movements.

"Just like it should be," Rachel agreed.
The ballet went perfectly, and at the
end the audience applauded wildly. The
girls curtsied, left the stage, and went to
join their proud parents. Kirsty, on the
other hand, rushed over to the side of
the stage.

"Thank you, Melodie," she said gratefully. "You saved our party."

"No, thank you!" Melodie beamed. "Without you, there would be no music at the king and queen's anniversary party. Please keep an eye out for more of Jack Frost's goblins."

"We will," Rachel and Kirsty promised together.

Melodie blew them each a kiss. "Good luck," she said. With a wave of her wand and a shower of twinkling lights, the fairy flew away.

Smiling happily, Rachel and Kirsty made their way to the hall to enjoy the rest of the party.

"I hope we meet more Party Fairies," Rachel said.

"Oh, I'm sure we will," replied Kirsty. Then she grinned. "As long as we keep going to parties!" she added.

Cherry and Melodie have their magic
party bags back. Next, Rachel
and Kirsty need to help

Grace

the Glitter Fairy!

Join their next adventure
in this special sneak peek. . . .

A Party Plan

"Isn't it a beautiful day?" Kirsty Tate said happily, looking up at the deep blue sky. "I'm so glad you're staying here for a whole week, Rachel."

Kirsty was sitting on the grass in the Tates' backyard, making a daisy chain with her best friend, Rachel Walker. Pearl, Kirsty's black-and-white kitten, was snoozing in a patch of sunshine in the middle of the path.

"You know, Rachel," Kirsty went on, picking another daisy. "This is the perfect day for—"

"A party!" Rachel broke in, knowing exactly what Kirsty was going to say.

Kirsty nodded, a frown on her face. "Let's hope Jack Frost's goblins don't spoil someone's special day."

"The Party Fairies will do their best to stop them," Rachel replied, sounding determined. "And so will we."

"Well," Kirsty said, adding another daisy to her chain, "we'll just have to keep our eyes open."

"And our ears," added Rachel.

Suddenly, there was a rustling behind

the fence. "OW!" someone muttered. "That hurt."

"Who was that?" gasped Rachel. "Do you think it was a goblin?"

Kirsty grinned and shook her head. "It's OK," she said. "It sounds like Mr. Cooper, our next-door neighbor."

At that moment, Mr. Cooper popped his head over the fence. He was a tall, thin man with a cheerful smile. "Sorry, Kirsty," he said, "did I startle you? I pricked my finger on the rosebush." He held up a small package wrapped in shiny blue paper. "I'm trying to hide these presents around our yard for the treasure hunt this afternoon."

"Treasure hunt?" repeated Rachel, looking puzzled.

Mr. Cooper nodded. "Yes, it's my son Jamie's birthday today," he replied. "He's five and we're having a party."

A party! Rachel and Kirsty glanced at each other in excitement.

RAINBOW magic™

There's Magic in Every Series!

The Rainbow Fairies

The Weather Fairies

The Jewel Fairies

The Pet Fairies

The Fun Day Fairies

The Petal Fairies

The Dance Fairies

The Music Fairies

The Sports Fairies

The Party Fairies

Read them all!

■ SCHOLASTIC

www.scholastic.com

www.rainbowmagiconline.com

HIT entertainment

RMFAIRY2

RAINBOW magic™

SPECIAL EDITION

Three Books in One—
More Rainbow Magic Fun!

■SCHOLASTIC

www.scholastic.com
www.rainbowmagiconline.com

HiT entertainment

RMSPECIAL4

RAINBOW magic

These activities are magical!
Play dress-up, send friendship notes, and much more!

◼SCHOLASTIC
www.scholastic.com
www.rainbowmagiconline.com

HiT entertainment

RMACTIV3

Perfectly Princess

Don't miss these royal adventures!

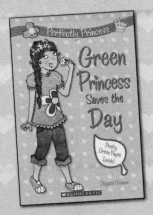

Printed on colored pages!